TUTU

THE ^*almost* HEMINGWAY CAT

Art

David Laughlin

Story

David L. Sloan

PHANTOM **PRESS**
K E Y W E S T

For use of information contained as source material, credit: David L. Sloan, author, and David Laughlin, illustrator, Tutu — The (almost) Hemingway Cat.

Editing services: dorothydrennen.com

Inquiries: david@phantompress.com

ISBN: 978-0-9831671-4-3

Thank you: Diamond Dave Gonzales — the cat's meow.

A cat has absolute emotional honesty: human beings, for one reason or another, may hide their feelings, but a cat does not.

- Ernest Miller Hemingway

TUTU

almost
THE ^ HEMINGWAY CAT

A KEY WEST STORYBOOK

The Florida Keys are ruled by several gangs of freewheeling cats. Though the names and faces change, one of these gangs has reigned supreme for more than 50 years. They are:

The Hemingway Cats.

THE ISLAND of K

1. The Hemingway Cats
2. The Duval Divas
3. Higgs Beach Hissers
4. The Petronia Persians
5. William Street Wailers
6. Fleming Street Fleabags
7. Porter House Paw Patrol
8. Southernmost Sassy Paws
9. Cow Key Kittens
10. Meowory Squares
11. The Key Lime Kitties
12. Garrison Bight Gatos
13. Soto's Tightrope Tom's
14. Mr. Winkers
15. East Martello Mousers

Once upon a time, on the shrimp docks of Livestock Island, a very special kitten was born.

She lived in an old bait bucket, and though she was definitely a cat, there was something different about her.

Her feet and her nose and her whiskers and toes – they looked like typical cat parts. But the fur around her waist had a mind of its own and stuck out like a big ballerina dress.

The names Anna Pavlova and Natalia Makarova were already taken, so this kitten was simply named Tutu.

And from the day she was born, Tutu knew that she was going to be a Hemingway Cat.

One morning when she was playing by the scrapyard on Shrimp Road, The Junkyard Dog made fun of her unruly fur.

But Tutu didn't care what The Junkyard Dog thought. Instead, she raised her head proudly and said, "I'm going to be a Hemingway Cat."

The Junkyard dog laughed.

And laughed.

And laughed.

Later that day she saw Lola the Lobster behind the Rusty Anchor. Lola the Lobster teased her too.

But Tutu didn't mind. She just smiled politely and told Lola the Lobster, "I'm going to be a Hemingway Cat."

Lola the Lobster laughed.

And laughed.

And laughed.

That evening as she was returning to her home, Tutu encountered the cat they call John Travolta.

The cat they call John Travolta taunted her more than any other animals.

But Tutu didn't cry. She curtsied to the cat they call John Travolta and said, "I'm going to be a Hemingway Cat."

The cat they call John Travolta

laughed.

And laughed.

And laughed.

All of the animals thought Tutu was crazy. No cat had ever left Livestock Island. But Tutu knew that what she said was true. She was going to be a Hemingway Cat.

One morning while Tutu was eating fresh shrimp tails on the dock by Captain Aller's Sun Scupper, Mr. Pelican landed next to her and made fun of Tutu's crazy fur.

Tutu pretended not to hear him. And when she finished the delicious shrimp tail she was eating, she looked at Mr. Pelican and said, "I m going to be a Hemingway Cat."

Mr. Pelican laughed.

And laughed.

And laughed.

"A Hemingway Cat?" he asked. "But The Hemingway Home is miles away. You would surely not survive the journey. But if you climb on my back, I will fly you there so you can see for yourself that you are nothing like the great Hemingway Cats living at the Whitehead Street Estate."

Tutu climbed on Mr. Pelican's back and they flew high up above the shrimp docks of Livestock Island.

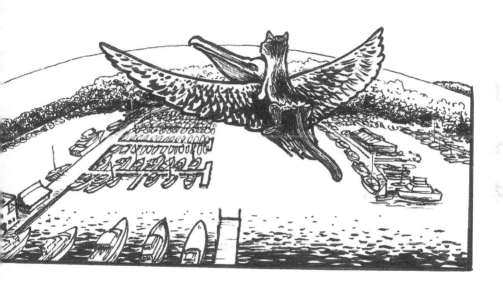

And they soared past the hawks of Mount Trashmore.

And they soared into Key West over the houseboats at Panariello Point.

And when they were high above the roosters at Blue Heaven, Tutu saw their destination.

And they landed at the foot of the Lighthouse on Whitehead Street.

Tutu hopped off of Mr. Pelican's back and stared across the street. Before her stood The Ernest Hemingway Home that she had only heard about in stories.

"That's my new home!" she squealed, bounding toward the house.

Mr. Pelican laughed and flew away. "They'll never let you be a Hemingway Cat!" he called out.

Tutu ran beside the long brick wall and then strutted right through the front gate.

A group of cats was gathered around the big water fountain. Tutu approached them and said, "My name is Tutu. I'm here to be a Hemingway Cat."

And the Hemingway Cats laughed.

And laughed.

And laughed.

"You can't be a Hemingway Cat," said a handsome tuxedo tabby. "Just look how small your paws are."

Another made fun of the big ring of fur around Tutu's waist.

But all of the cats fell respectfully silent when Eight Toe Alice appeared.

Eight Toe Alice looked Tutu up and down and said, "It takes more than good looks to be a Hemingway Cat, young kitten. You can't just decide to be one. You have to be born this way."

The other Hemingway Cats purred and put their noses up in the air.

"The very first Hemingway Cat was my great, great, great, great, great, great, great grandmother, Snow White," Eight Toe Alice explained.

"She was the daughter of Snowball, a good luck cat owned by Captain Stanley Dexter."

"What is a good luck cat?"
Tutu asked.

Eight Toe Alice held her giant paw in the air to show off each of the eight toes on it. "A good luck cat is a cat that has six toes or more on their front paw," she explained. "We bring good luck to sea captains, so for years we have traveled with them on their ships."

"Ernest Hemingway was fascinated with good luck cats and wanted one of his own. That is how Snow White came to live here. And now, every cat here is descended from her. So no matter how hard you try, kid, you will never be a Hemingway Cat."

The other Hemingway Cats
laughed.

And laughed.

And laughed.

Tutu looked down and counted her toes. 1. 2. 3. 4. 5. "Maybe I'm not a Hemingway Cat?" she thought.

As they pushed her out the gate onto Olivia Street, Tutu climbed up on the old brick wall and started to cry.

She cried.

And cried.

And cried.

Until her little whiskers looked like they were soaked with drops of rain.

And then she slept.

And slept.

And slept.

But even in her sleep, Tutu was haunted by voices telling her she would never be a Hemingway Cat.

Then Tutu felt a hand gently stroking her neck. And she opened her eyes to see a plump, jolly lady opening the camera app on her phone.

"Look, Martha! It's a Hemingway Cat!" the jolly lady exclaimed.

A family from Australia overheard her and rushed to the wall so they could photograph Tutu too. Soon there were a dozen people waiting for their turn to scratch between Tutu's ears and dry away her tears.

That night, the human boys who lived across the street brought Tutu some shrimp tails and a bowl of milk.

The next morning she awoke to a tray of kitty croissants from the bakery around the bend.

When she finished eating, Tutu climbed up on the wall of The Hemingway Home, and spent the entire day lazing in the sun as the tourists pointed to her and said she was the prettiest Hemingway Cat they had ever seen.

At first, the other Hemingway Cats were jealous, but Tutu never said a mean word to them.

Pretty soon, they all became friends.

Tutu would tell them of her adventures on Livestock Island, and they would tell her tales of The Great Snowball and his adventures at sea.

And then one day, Eight Toe Alice asked Tutu if she would like to come live behind the walls and be the very first honorary Hemingway Cat.

Tutu thanked Eight Toe Alice, but said, "No."

By now, Tutu was the most petted, most photographed, best fed, best scratched, and most pampered cat on the entire block. And she was okay with that.

And though she isn't descended from Snow Ball, this special little kitty cat couldn't be happier, simply being Tutu — The (almost) Hemingway Cat.

Remember: Dreams don't always work out like we planned. Sometimes they work out better.

Story by David L. Sloan

Illustrations by David Laughlin

Tutu: The *almost* ^ Hemingway Cat

Made in the USA
Lexington, KY
14 May 2016